My First Acrostic
ALL ABOUT ME

Amazing Acrostics
Edited By Jenni Harrison

First published in Great Britain in 2020 by:

Young Writers
Remus House
Coltsfoot Drive
Peterborough
PE2 9BF
Telephone: 01733 890066
Website: www.youngwriters.co.uk

All Rights Reserved
Book Design by Ashley Janson
© Copyright Contributors 2019
Softback ISBN 978-1-83928-630-8

Printed and bound in the UK by BookPrintingUK
Website: www.bookprintinguk.com
YB0431A

Dear Reader,

Dear Reader,

Welcome to a fun-filled book of acrostic poems!

Here at Young Writers, we are delighted to introduce our new poetry competition for KS1 pupils, *My First Acrostic: All About Me*. Acrostic poems are an enjoyable way to introduce pupils to the world of poetry and allow the young writer to open their imagination to a range of topics of their choice. The colourful and engaging entry forms allowed even the youngest (or most reluctant) of pupils to create a poem using the acrostic technique, and with that, encouraged them to include other literary techniques such as similes and description. Here at Young Writers we are passionate about introducing the love and art of creative writing to the next generation and we love being a part of their journey.

From pets to family, from hobbies to idols, these pupils have shaped and crafted their ideas brilliantly, showcasing their budding creativity. So, we invite you to proceed through these pages and take a glimpse into these blossoming young writers' minds. We hope you will relish these poems as much as we have.

Contents

Aviemore Primary School, Muirton

Hanna Drozd (6)	1
Lochlan Gordon McAllister (6)	2
Jack Stewart (7)	3
Josh Murphy (7)	4
Olivia Robinson (7)	5
Filip Grojec (7)	6
Amdad Miah (7)	7
Rileigh Maureen Beattie (7)	8
Ciaran Lambie (8)	9
Ross Adamson (7)	10
Torin Amos (7)	11
Noah White (7)	12
Maja Ponska (6)	13
Kaleb Irvine (7)	14
Joe Thurlow (7)	15

Bishop Henderson CE Primary School, Taunton

Isabella Mae Payne (5)	16
Ava Norman (6)	17
Nevaeh Pope (6)	18
Sienna Pope (6)	19
Rosie Date (7) & Lola	20
Heidi Belle Cook (5)	21
Jephiya Elizabeth Joice (5)	22
Zara Coles (5)	23

Dingle Community Primary School, Kingswinford

Nikitha Thusyanthan (7)	24
Archie Broome (5)	25
Mohammad Alazizi (6)	26
Talliah Gordon (5)	27
Oliwia Wenta (6)	28
Charlie Lowin (6)	29
Kieran Hassall (5)	30
Evie Elwell (6)	31
Poppy Elizabeth Turley (6)	32
Sofia Tynan (6)	33
Olivia Hemming (5)	34
Joshua Ellwood (5)	35
Sofia Edwards (5)	36
Leo Healey (6)	37
Megan Jade Moseley (5)	38
Tia-Grace Billingham (5)	39
Rhys Kirkham (5)	40

High Legh Primary School, High Legh

Malayka Eva Waheed (6)	41
Jack Waring (7)	42

Normanton House School, Derby

Mariam Nazir (7)	43
Juweriya Shakeel (5)	44
Nawal Salman (7)	45
Khadijah Bint-Naeem (7)	46
Warisha Shahzad (7)	47
Raafe Bin-Naeem (6)	48
Husna Zaman (7)	49

Haseeb Ahmed (6)	50

Northumberland Heath Primary School, Erith

Sangari K (6)	51
Skye Rackstraw (6)	52
Sidney Louise Cox (6)	53
Paulina Zurauskaite (6)	54
Taysia Fender (6)	55
Sienna Powell (6)	56
Nyomi Ofurhie (6)	57
Adi Gimziunas (6)	58
Bobby F (6)	59
Ivy R (7)	60
Precious B (6)	61
Oskaras R (6)	62
Amelia Laughland-Reed (6)	63
Peyton S (6)	64
Sofia Mitova (6)	65
Harry Prior (6)	66
Bhavjeet Singh Araich (6)	67
Tommy W (6)	68
Tayo Stephen Oluyomi (6)	69
Jem Tektas (6)	70
Tegan Alicia Isabella Daly (6)	71
Raiens Grietins (6)	72
Rico (6)	73
Holly Grace (6)	74
Maria M (7)	75
Reggie James Gill (6)	76
Shelby (6), Joshua, Shane, Ryan & Tyler (7)	77
Macey-Rose Johnson (6)	78
Stevan A (6)	79
Henley Reading (6)	80
Jack Wilkinson-Chandler (6)	81
Ethan A (6)	82
Ryan-Lee Richards (6)	83
Tate E (6)	84
Johnny Oheneba Odoi-Kyene (6)	85
Mohammed Ayaan Zaheer (6)	86

Oakwood Primary School, Cheltenham

Skye Sutherland-Trowbridge (7)	87
Noela Bray (7)	88
Rebeca Craciun (6)	89
Richie-Jae Alistair David Smith (6)	90
Julia Worobec (5)	91
Rowan Haddon (5)	92
Honey-Rose McConnon (6)	93

St Mary's CE Academy Walkley, Sheffield

Isaac Andrew (7)	94
Nuri Bennaser (5)	95
Zeenat Ahmadi (6)	96
Dominic Gregory (5)	97

The Gates Primary School, Westhoughton

Abigail Ali (6)	98
Tristan Forshaw (6)	99
Isabelle Travers (7)	100
Rosie Ellis-Poole (6)	101
Jack Price (7)	102
Lucy Evans (7)	103
Harris Longworth (5)	104
Imogen Price (7)	105
Emmy Melia (6)	106
Ire Ahmed Yusuff (5)	107
Max Matthews (6)	108
Max Partington (6)	109
Leo Joseph Lannon (6)	110
Stephanie Strood (7)	111
Freya Johnson (6)	112
Jazmin Apple Hill (6)	113
Ava Rose Brindley (6)	114
Dakota Jackson (6)	115
Lola Taylor (6)	116
Zara Poppy Jones (5)	117
Keiji Gregory (6)	118
Heidi Richardson (6)	119

Justin B (6)	120
Oliver Procter (6)	121
Alex Miles Stephens (6)	122
Ethan Scott (6)	123
Ethan Brandwood (6)	124
Ruby May Walker (5)	125
Chloe Kearsley (5)	126
Junior James McWhinnie (6)	127
George Shaw (5)	128
Emily Fletcher (5)	129
Harry Mylrea (5)	130
Amelia Eaves (6)	131
Caitlin Emelia Holden-Green (5)	132
Zakariya Jones (5)	133

Woodlands School, Great Warley

Brianna Olaniyi-Edwards (6)	134
Lucas Oluitan (6)	135
Arya Patel (6)	136

Woodlands School Hutton Manor, Hutton

William Marx (5)	137
Mia Isabel Jordan (6)	138
Thomas Howells (5)	139
Annie Barke (6)	140
Heath Lenz (6)	141
Beth Currie (6)	142
Penelope Kettle (6)	143
Zachary Hill (5)	144
Jamie Murphy (6)	145
Florence Bray (7)	146
Scarlett George (6)	147
Harry Carr (7)	148

The Poems

Yourek

Y ourek is a cuddly dog.
O ver the field he runs.
U p the stairs he goes.
R uns very fast.
E ats everything.
K etchup is what he likes licking.

Hanna Drozd (6)
Aviemore Primary School, Muirton

World

W orld is a planet.
O bject is a thing you can see.
R acing is like a marathon.
L ochlan is a name.
D og is a pet.

Lochlan Gordon McAllister (6)
Aviemore Primary School, Muirton

Javelin

J ourney of the javelin.
A dventure.
V ery far.
E njoy.
L ike it.
I t is good.
N ice.

Jack Stewart (7)
Aviemore Primary School, Muirton

Squash

S quash is amazing!
Q uiet.
U sing
A racket.
S quash.
H ot pizza at the end.

Josh Murphy (7)
Aviemore Primary School, Muirton

Farms

F armers are fantastic at feeding
A nimals.
R are breeds.
M ake food.
S its carefully.

Olivia Robinson (7)
Aviemore Primary School, Muirton

Pizza

P izza is yummy.
I like it.
Z ig zag cheese.
Z ero mushrooms.
A pizza is amazing.

Filip Grojec (7)
Aviemore Primary School, Muirton

Amdad

A nimals have homes.
M arch is my birthday.
D oor.
A bout.
D ad is working.

Amdad Miah (7)
Aviemore Primary School, Muirton

Easter

E aster eggs.
A ctive.
S pring.
T ea tree.
E aster.
R iding.

Rileigh Maureen Beattie (7)
Aviemore Primary School, Muirton

Food

F eels good.
O ats are food.
O il can go in food.
D airy cheese and milk are food.

Ciaran Lambie (8)
Aviemore Primary School, Muirton

Alien

A lot of heads.
L egs.
I t has a lot of eyes.
E ffect.
N ot nice.

Ross Adamson (7)
Aviemore Primary School, Muirton

Nesa

N ice and quiet.
E xcellent listener.
S mooth as silk.
A mazing dog.

Torin Amos (7)
Aviemore Primary School, Muirton

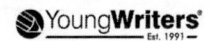

Spike

S urprise.
P uffs up.
I nterrupting.
K ind.
E xcellent.

Noah White (7)
Aviemore Primary School, Muirton

Apple

A round.
P ick.
P eel.
L ove.
E at.

Maja Ponska (6)
Aviemore Primary School, Muirton

Game

G reat
A bout
M onsters
E veryone likes.

Kaleb Irvine (7)
Aviemore Primary School, Muirton

Joe

J oyful.
O utgoing.
E xcellent.

Joe Thurlow (7)
Aviemore Primary School, Muirton

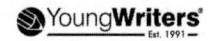

Swinging Smiles

M y favourite thing to do.
O ne hand at a time.
N o looking down.
K eeping hanging on like an orangutan.
E xercise is good for me.
Y ou have to be brave.

B ackwards and forwards.
A crobats are clever.
R ace to the end.
S trong arms help me hang.

Isabella Mae Payne (5)
Bishop Henderson CE Primary School, Taunton

Ice Cream

I like ice cream.
C hildren have it at the beach.
E veryone likes it.

C hildren choose different flavours.
R ainbow colours.
E normous beach to eat ice cream.
A nd they are yummy.
M y poem is finished.

Ava Norman (6)
Bishop Henderson CE Primary School, Taunton

Dinosaur

D inosaurs are my favourite.
I love dinosaurs and T-rexes.
N oisy dinosaurs.
O range dinosaurs.
S cary dinosaurs.
A wesome dinosaurs.
U nbelievable dinosaurs.
R oar like a dinosaur.

Nevaeh Pope (6)
Bishop Henderson CE Primary School, Taunton

Unicorn Dreams

U nicorns are my favourite.
N ice and sparkly.
I love unicorns.
C ute and cuddly.
O n top of the clouds.
R ainbow unicorns.
N ight-time flying in the stars.

Sienna Pope (6)
Bishop Henderson CE Primary School, Taunton

School

S chool is super successful.
C aring for each other.
H appy and joyful.
O ur school is amazing!
O ur school is full of brilliant teachers.
L iving life to its fullness.

Rosie Date (7) & Lola
Bishop Henderson CE Primary School, Taunton

Heidi

H appy, funny, kind and helpful.
E veryone is my friend.
I love holding baby Sophie.
D addy, Mummy, Lottie and baby are my family.
I love to play at the park.

Heidi Belle Cook (5)
Bishop Henderson CE Primary School, Taunton

Cats

C ats are loving pets.
A mazingly, they have a super sense of smell.
T he claws of a cat are super sharp.
S uper duper fluffy fur makes cats super cute.

Jephiya Elizabeth Joice (5)
Bishop Henderson CE Primary School, Taunton

Cat

C ats are cuddly.
A ll cats drink milk.
T he cat's tail is furry.

Zara Coles (5)
Bishop Henderson CE Primary School, Taunton

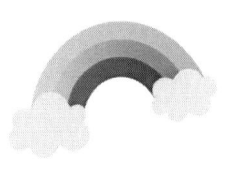

Nikitha

N umber 7 is my favourite.
I ndependent colouring.
K ind to my friends.
I like playing with Barbie.
T aking turns in games.
H elpful for my mum.
A pples are my favourite.

Nikitha Thusyanthan (7)
Dingle Community Primary School, Kingswinford

Archie

A lways kind.
R ed is my favourite colour.
C aring to my friends and family.
H appy.
I ndependent learning.
E xcited when playing.

Archie Broome (5)
Dingle Community Primary School, Kingswinford

Mohammad

M aking friends.
O n the park
H aving fun.
A lways running.
M aths
M usic
A nd
D ancing make me feel happy.

Mohammad Alazizi (6)
Dingle Community Primary School, Kingswinford

Talliah

T aking turns.
A pples I like.
L ove my daddy.
L ove my guinea pigs.
I ndoors.
A nd at
H ome.

Talliah Gordon (5)
Dingle Community Primary School, Kingswinford

Oliwia

O n a swing.
L ooking for birds
I n the park.
W onderful excitement.
I ce cream time.
A lways happy.

Oliwia Wenta (6)
Dingle Community Primary School, Kingswinford

Charlie

C lever.
H appy.
A lways climbs.
R unning.
L ikes football.
I nto sport.
E ating pizza.

Charlie Lowin (6)
Dingle Community Primary School, Kingswinford

Kieran

K icks a football
I nto the goal.
E veryone cheers.
R unning around.
A lways smiling.
N ever sad.

Kieran Hassall (5)
Dingle Community Primary School, Kingswinford

Evie

E nergetic when I wake up.
V ery happy when writing a story.
I nterested in non-fiction books.
E xcited every day.

Evie Elwell (6)
Dingle Community Primary School, Kingswinford

Poppy

P olite to my friends.
O n top of the mountain.
P laying with my toys.
P ink, I love.
Y ummy carrots.

Poppy Elizabeth Turley (6)
Dingle Community Primary School, Kingswinford

Sofia

S kipping at the park.
O n the trampoline.
F un with my cousins.
I n the sunshine.
A lways smiling.

Sofia Tynan (6)
Dingle Community Primary School, Kingswinford

Olivia

O ranges.
L ikes bananas.
I nside.
V ery happy.
I love friends
A nd family.

Olivia Hemming (5)
Dingle Community Primary School, Kingswinford

Joshua

J umping
O n tyres.
S haring toys.
H ouse rules.
U s time
A t the park.

Joshua Ellwood (5)
Dingle Community Primary School, Kingswinford

Sofia

S miling.
O n the park.
F riendly.
I nteresting.
A lways happy.

Sofia Edwards (5)
Dingle Community Primary School, Kingswinford

Leo

L ikes monkeys at the zoo.
E xcited about gorillas.
O range is my favourite colour.

Leo Healey (6)
Dingle Community Primary School, Kingswinford

Megan

M ermaids.
E lephants.
G iraffes.
A nd all things
N ice.

Megan Jade Moseley (5)
Dingle Community Primary School, Kingswinford

Tia

T rampolining every day.
I like colouring
A nd playing with my Barbie dolls.

Tia-Grace Billingham (5)
Dingle Community Primary School, Kingswinford

Rhys

R uns fast.
H elpful.
Y ellow control.
S haring.

Rhys Kirkham (5)
Dingle Community Primary School, Kingswinford

The Unicorn Sprinkle

U nicorns are my favourite because they sparkle.
N ice and glittery.
I wish I could ride a unicorn.
C olourful unicorn hair is what I love.
O h! I love you, unicorn!
R ainbow and cutie marks are on unicorn skin.
N ow that is why I love my unicorn.

Malayka Eva Waheed (6)
High Legh Primary School, High Legh

Adventure

A wesome views.
D esigning dens.
V ery exciting!
E arwigs and millipedes.
N ew discoveries.
T ents and campfires.
U nder the stars.
R oaming the forest.
E xplore the world!

Jack Waring (7)
High Legh Primary School, High Legh

My Name

M y family are the best.
A lways looking out for others.
R eally like school.
I ce cream is my favourite food.
A lways helping others.
M y friends are the best.

N ow it is the best day ever.
A lways having fun.
Z am Zam is the best.
I like painting.
R eally high on the swings.

Mariam Nazir (7)
Normanton House School, Derby

My Dream Pet

U nique is all I seek.
N ice and clean. Never ever mean.
I t's so fluffy I'm gonna die!
C an you be my friend forever?
O ver the clouds, they fly so high.
R ainbow hair, making everyone stare.
N othing beats my beautiful pet, the most extraordinary animal I've ever met.

Juweriya Shakeel (5)
Normanton House School, Derby

Chocolatey Things

C hocolates are very sweet!
H ot chocolates are tasty. Yummy!
O h! I burnt my tongue.
C heers me up!
O n a chocolate shop.
L ive with chocolate.
A pples with chocolate on top.
T ea time with chocolate.
E very day I eat chocolate.

Nawal Salman (7)
Normanton House School, Derby

The Noisy Unicorns

U nicorns are mostly white.
N o one has seen a unicorn.
I like flying unicorns.
C olourful wings look so nice.
O n his head is a shiny horn.
R unning and jumping, here and there.
N aughty and noisy, making all of us happy.

Khadijah Bint-Naeem (7)
Normanton House School, Derby

Unicorn

U nderstands my every word.
N eon coloured mane.
I n a magical land, it gallops.
C andy is its favourite treat.
O ver a magical rainbow, it flies.
R ocky paths glimmer where it trots.
N eighing everywhere it goes.

Warisha Shahzad (7)
Normanton House School, Derby

Horse

H aving strong legs to run fast.
O n its neck, long and fluffy hair.
R unning just like a cheetah.
S o nice and loyal.
E veryone likes to have one.

Raafe Bin-Naeem (6)
Normanton House School, Derby

Husna

Husna is a **H** appy girl.
Husna is **U** nique.
Husna likes **S** tars.
Husna likes **N** uts.
Husna likes **A** pples.

Husna Zaman (7)
Normanton House School, Derby

I Play

I play in the park.

P irates, I like.
L ion, I am.
A ngry, I can be.
Y oung, I am.

Haseeb Ahmed (6)
Normanton House School, Derby

Truth

T elling the truth to your friends and teachers, and be nice.

R espect your friends and teachers, and be kind.

U se your school rules, and when a teacher tells you to do something you have to do it.

T aking care of your friends and when someone falls over you have to tell the teacher, and when someone hits you, you don't have to hit them back.

H onesty is the best policy.

Sangari K (6)
Northumberland Heath Primary School, Erith

Truth

T ell the truth to your family, and they will tell the truth to you.
R espect makes me feel happy because my friends tell the truth to me.
U nder a colourful rainbow, it makes me feel happy and kind.
T ell the truth to anybody.
H onesty is helpful, kind, and nice.

Skye Rackstraw (6)
Northumberland Heath Primary School, Erith

Truth

T elling the truth to Santa.
R ainbows make me feel happy.
U nicorns remind me of when I wake up in the morning and see my family.
T ell the truth to the Easter Bunny.
H elping each other and being kind to each other.

Sidney Louise Cox (6)
Northumberland Heath Primary School, Erith

Truth

T elling the truth to your parents is important.
R ainbow is a happy colour.
U nicorns make people happy and they are sparkly.
T ruth smells like yummy dog food.
H elping people when they are hurt because it is kind!

Paulina Zurauskaite (6)
Northumberland Heath Primary School, Erith

Truth

T elling the truth is kind and excellent.
R espect is wonderful and good.
U nderstanding the truth is good.
T wo of the best things are honesty and happiness.
H elping each other is excellent and amazing.

Taysia Fender (6)
Northumberland Heath Primary School, Erith

Truth

T ell the truth and never lie.
R espect others and never lie.
U se the truth, because you should never lie.
T ell people you should never lie to people.
H elp your friends to tell the truth all day.

Sienna Powell (6)
Northumberland Heath Primary School, Erith

Truth

T ell the truth to your mum and dad.
R emember to tell the truth.
U nlikely you wouldn't tell the truth.
T elling the truth is lovely.
H onesty is good because it is good to tell the truth.

Nyomi Ofurhie (6)
Northumberland Heath Primary School, Erith

Truth

T elling the truth is good, remember.
R espect and truth is a big gift.
U nderstanding the truth is lovely and kind.
T elling the truth is good and honest.
H appiness feels like the truth.

Adi Gimziunas (6)
Northumberland Heath Primary School, Erith

Truth

T ell your teacher the truth every day.
R espect everyone, and always your friends.
U nderstand good listening
T ake care of your friends and teacher.
H onesty is the best policy.

Bobby F (6)
Northumberland Heath Primary School, Erith

Truth

T ell your teacher and friends the truth.
R espect everyone around you.
U nderstand all your school rules.
T alk to everyone that you can trust.
H onesty is the best policy.

Ivy R (7)
Northumberland Heath Primary School, Erith

Truth

T ell the truth always.
R emember to tell the truth every day.
U nderstand how to be honest.
T ell your friends to always tell the truth.
H onest is the best thing to be.

Precious B (6)
Northumberland Heath Primary School, Erith

Truth

T ell the truth to your peers and teachers.
R espect each other and your teachers.
U nderstand what the word truth means.
T alk with manners.
H onesty is the best policy.

Oskaras R (6)
Northumberland Heath Primary School, Erith

Truth

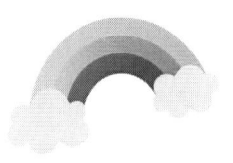

T ell the truth even if you are in trouble.
R espect your friends and teachers.
U nderstand if they're sad or not.
T ake responsibility.
H onesty is the best policy.

Amelia Laughland-Reed (6)
Northumberland Heath Primary School, Erith

Truth

T ell the truth to a teacher.
R espect your teacher.
U nderstand what the teacher in class wants.
T ake care of the people in your class.
H onesty is the best policy.

Peyton S (6)
Northumberland Heath Primary School, Erith

Truth

T hink about telling the truth to Santa.
R emnants of shiny rainbows.
U nicorns are beautiful and sparkly.
T ell the person to say the truth.
H eroes say the truth.

Sofia Mitova (6)
Northumberland Heath Primary School, Erith

Truth

T ell the truth always.
R espect your teacher always.
U nderstand your behaviour.
T ell other people who aren't honest.
H onesty is the best policy.

Harry Prior (6)
Northumberland Heath Primary School, Erith

Truth

T ell the truth every day.
R emember to tell the truth.
U nderstand what the truth means.
T rust your friends every magnificent day.
H onest is a good thing to be.

Bhavjeet Singh Araich (6)
Northumberland Heath Primary School, Erith

Truth

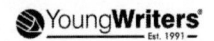

T ell the truth always.
R espect others the same.
U nderstand your actions.
T ake your actions seriously.
H elp others the same as you want to be helped.

Tommy W (6)
Northumberland Heath Primary School, Erith

Truth

T he truth is brilliant.
R ealise that being honest is great.
U se the truth so people believe you.
T he best idea is the truth.
H onesty is fantastic.

Tayo Stephen Oluyomi (6)
Northumberland Heath Primary School, Erith

Truth

T he truth is good.
R especting the teachers.
U nderstanding how people feel.
T elling lies is naughty.
H ey! Why aren't you telling the truth?

Jem Tektas (6)
Northumberland Heath Primary School, Erith

Truth

T ell the truth.
R espect others, how you want them to treat you.
U nderstand other people.
T ake care of others.
H onesty is the best policy.

Tegan Alicia Isabella Daly (6)
Northumberland Heath Primary School, Erith

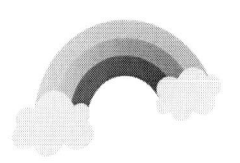

Truth

T ap the man on the shoulder.
R oll the green ball said the child.
U nhappy is bad.
T ell the truth said Mrs E.
H onesty is helping children.

Raiens Grietins (6)
Northumberland Heath Primary School, Erith

Truth

T elling the truth is nice.
R especting others gives you a prize.
U nderstanding is important.
T rying your best.
H elping for the rest.

Rico (6)
Northumberland Heath Primary School, Erith

Truth

T elling the truth is kind.
R ainbows are colourful.
U nicorns are colourful.
T elling the truth is kind.
H appy people tell the truth.

Holly Grace (6)
Northumberland Heath Primary School, Erith

Truth

T ell the truth to the teacher.
R espect everyone.
U nderstand the rules.
T ell people to tell the truth.
H onesty is the best policy.

Maria M (7)
Northumberland Heath Primary School, Erith

Truth

T elling the truth to Santa.
R espect your family.
U nicorns are beautiful.
T ell the truth to Jesus.
H onesty is a nice word.

Reggie James Gill (6)
Northumberland Heath Primary School, Erith

Truth

T ap on the shoulder.
R emember to be nice.
U nderstand kindness.
T ell the truth to your friends.
H appy to see your family.

Shelby (6), Joshua, Shane, Ryan & Tyler (7)
Northumberland Heath Primary School, Erith

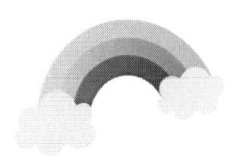

Truth

T ell the teacher the truth.
R espect the teacher.
U se your words.
T ake care of your work.
H onesty is about what you did.

Macey-Rose Johnson (6)
Northumberland Heath Primary School, Erith

Truth

T ell the truth.
R espect your friends.
U nderstand what is the truth.
T ake care of yourself.
H onesty is the best policy.

Stevan A (6)
Northumberland Heath Primary School, Erith

Truth

T elling the truth to your friends is kind.
R espect your family.
U nderstand your friends.
T o be truthful.
H onesty.

Henley Reading (6)
Northumberland Heath Primary School, Erith

Truth

T ell the truth.
R ealise the truth.
U nderstand the truth.
T ell kids the truth.
H onesty is the key to the truth.

Jack Wilkinson-Chandler (6)
Northumberland Heath Primary School, Erith

Truth

T ell people the truth.
R espect everyone.
U nderstand the truth.
T ell the truth.
H onesty is the best policy.

Ethan A (6)
Northumberland Heath Primary School, Erith

Truth

T ap on the shoulder.
R emember to be nice.
U nderstand the truth.
T ell the truth.
H appy to see your family.

Ryan-Lee Richards (6)
Northumberland Heath Primary School, Erith

Truth

T ell the teacher.
R espect everyone.
U nderstand truth.
T ake care of yourself.
H onesty is the best policy.

Tate E (6)
Northumberland Heath Primary School, Erith

Truth

T ell the truth.
R espect the teacher.
U se your manners.
T ake responsibility.
H ave nice manners.

Johnny Oheneba Odoi-Kyene (6)
Northumberland Heath Primary School, Erith

Truth

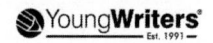

T urn around.
R ain is coming.
U nhappy isn't happy.
T o the house.
H ey! Open the door!

Mohammed Ayaan Zaheer (6)
Northumberland Heath Primary School, Erith

Birthday

B lowing out candles.
I cing on the cake.
R ipping the wrapping paper off presents.
T he treats and music make me happy.
H aving fun at my birthday party.
D ancing with my friends.
A ll of us having a fantastic time.
Y esterday I was six, and today I am celebrating being seven!

Skye Sutherland-Trowbridge (7)
Oakwood Primary School, Cheltenham

About Legoland

L ots of fun.
E veryone queuing.
G o! Go! Go! My turn now.
O ff we go, on to the next one.
L aughing and talking with my family.
A dventure time, checking my map.
N ow it's time to go home.
D riving and singing until I fall asleep.

Noela Bray (7)
Oakwood Primary School, Cheltenham

Ice Cream

I like to eat ice cream.
C ats are my favourite animals.
E veryone plays with me.

C hocolate is the best.
R ainbows are very colourful.
E lephants are big mammals.
A t break, I eat my snack.
M y mum makes delicious treats.

Rebeca Craciun (6)
Oakwood Primary School, Cheltenham

Holidays

H aving fun
O n the beach.
L aughing all the time.
I ce cream is nice.
D ogs being walked.
A boat on the sea.
Y ellow sun smiling.
S ummer's great.

Richie-Jae Alistair David Smith (6)
Oakwood Primary School, Cheltenham

Unicorn

U mbrella when it rains.
N adia is my sister.
I love my pets.
C hocolate is my favourite.
O range is tasty.
R oller coaster ride.
N ight is for sleeping.

Julia Worobec (5)
Oakwood Primary School, Cheltenham

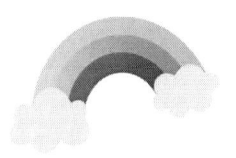

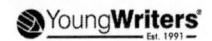

Trains

T homas is an engine.
R ailway tracks.
A nnie and Clarabell are carriages.
I sland of Sodor.
N ice views as you travel.
S team train.

Rowan Haddon (5)
Oakwood Primary School, Cheltenham

Santa

S anta rides a sleigh
A nd brings lots of toys.
N ow it's time for Christmas.
T he fun had just begun.
A nd all enjoy your day!

Honey-Rose McConnon (6)
Oakwood Primary School, Cheltenham

Crocodile

C reeping through the undergrowth.
R unning through the leaves.
O n its way to find its prey.
C lawing at the dirty soil.
O h! He has found a tasty treat!
D own, the snack goes down its throat.
I t made the crocodile splutter and choke.
L urking back to the riverbank.
E nding his journey across the jungle.

Isaac Andrew (7)
St Mary's CE Academy Walkley, Sheffield

Winter Poem

W inter is a season in the year.
I t is a time when you can get a cold.
N early everybody can get sick.
T ea will warm you up, for sure.
E at hot foods to keep toasty.
R ainy days may come ahead!

Nuri Bennaser (5)
St Mary's CE Academy Walkley, Sheffield

Summer

S mearing on suncream.
U nder the umbrella for shade.
M elting popsicles.
M assive waves.
E veryone happy.
R eady to play all day.

Zeenat Ahmadi (6)
St Mary's CE Academy Walkley, Sheffield

Space

S aturn has rings.
P luto is small.
A liens on Mars.
C omets whizz.
E arth is where we live.

Dominic Gregory (5)
St Mary's CE Academy Walkley, Sheffield

Blackpool

B lackpool Tower glows at night.
L ots of fireworks.
A lot of stars.
C olours in the air when fireworks are crashing.
K ites on the beach.
P eople's dogs running.
O n the beach, I can make sandcastles.
O n the game with money and prizes fall.
L ots of carriages and horses.

Abigail Ali (6)
The Gates Primary School, Westhoughton

Guinea Pigs

G orgeous.
U nscared.
I nto the conservatory to stroke them.
N ibbles.
E ating a lot.
A t breakfast, they go straight to their food.

P inching my fingers.
I nto the bedroom, they go.
G oing to sleep a lot.
S o cuddly.

Tristan Forshaw (6)
The Gates Primary School, Westhoughton

Gymnastics

G reat cartwheels into the splits.
Y ou have to be flexible.
M any types of flips.
N ever give up.
A wesome backbends.
S cary sometimes.
T he super splits.
I nto walk over.
C artwheels into splits.
S uper frog.

Isabelle Travers (7)
The Gates Primary School, Westhoughton

My Favourite Thing To Do

S aturday is the day I go.
W ater is fun to swim in.
I like to swim because it is fun.
M y class is at 9 o'clock.
M y class is on stage 4.
I wait on the bench.
N o swimming in milk!
G oing to swimming is fun!

Rosie Ellis-Poole (6)
The Gates Primary School, Westhoughton

Magic!

M agic hat.
A bunny pops out the hat.
G ames come out the hat.
I nside the hat.
C ats come from the hat.
I n the magician's hat.
A ll the magicians have a tall magic hat.
N o magician can help people.

Jack Price (7)
The Gates Primary School, Westhoughton

Seaside

S unny every day.
E verywhere you go is wonderful.
A lways a good view.
S andcastles are so fun to build.
I like going there.
D elicious ice cream to eat.
E xciting swimming in the deep, blue sea.

Lucy Evans (7)
The Gates Primary School, Westhoughton

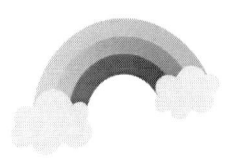

Brother Fletcher

F letcher is a cool boy.
L oopy Fletcher.
E ncouraging Fletcher.
T he roly-poly Fletcher.
C alm Fletcher.
H appy Fletcher.
E nergetic Fletcher.
R oaring Fletcher.

Harris Longworth (5)
The Gates Primary School, Westhoughton

My Favourite Thing To Do

R eading books is good.
E xcellent words in books.
A dventures to go on.
D escription is amazing.
I like new chapters.
N ew words to look up and learn.
G reat words to hear and learn.

Imogen Price (7)
The Gates Primary School, Westhoughton

My Cat

M eow!
I like his hum.
D ashes when visitors come over.
N oses around the room.
I s all green.
G reat friend.
H ot, light sunshine.
T ime in the dark.

Emmy Melia (6)
The Gates Primary School, Westhoughton

Sisters

S isters that love me.
I love my sisters.
S o, they were going to race.
T hey are beautiful.
E xcellent sisters.
R olling sisters.
S kating sisters on ice.

Ire Ahmed Yusuff (5)
The Gates Primary School, Westhoughton

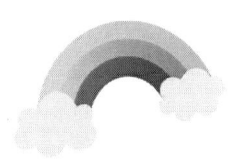

Drawing

D elightful colours.
R elaxing days.
A rt is fun.
W ater picture's fun.
I like to colour around shapes.
N ever stop colouring.
G reat colouring.

Max Matthews (6)
The Gates Primary School, Westhoughton

My Holiday

T he beach was covered with shells.
U nder the water blowing bubbles.
R eally hot and sunny.
K eep kicking the sand and shells.
E ating lots of ice cream.
Y um!

Max Partington (6)
The Gates Primary School, Westhoughton

The Seaside

S uch a good view.
E verywhere you see it.
A nimals everywhere.
S ea is so amazing.
I like to go there.
D elicious doughnuts.
E xciting swimming.

Leo Joseph Lannon (6)
The Gates Primary School, Westhoughton

My Country

U tterly sunny.
K eep shining sun!
R eally noisy market.
A lways going somewhere.
I ncredible places.
N arrow beams.
E njoying family time.

Stephanie Strood (7)
The Gates Primary School, Westhoughton

Holiday!

H ot weather.
O n the beach it is sandy.
L ots of sunshine.
I n the swimming pool.
D elicious ice cream.
A big sandcastle.
Y ummy food!

Freya Johnson (6)
The Gates Primary School, Westhoughton

Scooter

S uper fun.
C racking bumps.
O ne more racing.
O ne more speed.
T he awesome decoration.
E nding with stuff.
R acing up the hills.

Jazmin Apple Hill (6)
The Gates Primary School, Westhoughton

My Dog

T ough teeth.
I love messing with his fur.
T ries to eat his collar.
A lways a lazy daisy in the night.
N oisy and barks when people come in the house.

Ava Rose Brindley (6)
The Gates Primary School, Westhoughton

Autumn

A utumn pinches my phone.
U nusually furry dog.
T he dog is kind to me.
U p and down.
M y dog sleeps on my knees.
N aughty sometimes.

Dakota Jackson (6)
The Gates Primary School, Westhoughton

Paul

P erfect when I'm with him.
A mazing when I'm with him.
U nhappy when I'm not with him.
L oveable dad who cares about me and my sister Olivia.

Lola Taylor (6)
The Gates Primary School, Westhoughton

Madeline

M ostly happy.
A bit cheeky.
D addy loves her.
E nergetic.
L ikes to play.
I nteresting.
N ice.
E nergetic.

Zara Poppy Jones (5)
The Gates Primary School, Westhoughton

Games

G et out my Lego.
A loud Lego building crashing.
M assive Lego building.
E njoy the challenge.
S haring is fun.

Keiji Gregory (6)
The Gates Primary School, Westhoughton

Pizza

P epperoni is my favourite.
I t has got some on the pizza.
Z ip it in the bag.
Z ip it up quick.
A ll in a box.

Heidi Richardson (6)
The Gates Primary School, Westhoughton

Pizza

P izza is delicious.
I like cheese pizza.
Z ip up the bag.
Z *oom!* In the car.
A mazing!

Justin B (6)
The Gates Primary School, Westhoughton

Pizza

P epperoni pizza.
I like cheese pizza.
Z ooming.
Z ip in the bag.
A lways pizza on a Friday.

Oliver Procter (6)
The Gates Primary School, Westhoughton

Wogiy

W hiskers on her.
O n the chair all day.
G iggles.
I love Wogiy.
Y ummy! She likes food.

Alex Miles Stephens (6)
The Gates Primary School, Westhoughton

My Silly Daddy

D ad is funny.
A silly dad.
D ad is daft.
D ad always laughs.
Y es, he loves me a lot.

Ethan Scott (6)
The Gates Primary School, Westhoughton

My Sister

E rin is naughty.
R eally nice playing with me.
I like to play with her.
N oisy when I wake up.

Ethan Brandwood (6)
The Gates Primary School, Westhoughton

Mummy

M y mum sees me so much and she is awesome.
E xcited girl, laughs so much.
L ikes meat and she likes brown.

Ruby May Walker (5)
The Gates Primary School, Westhoughton

Quiet Mikey

M arvellous Mikey.
I love Mikey.
K ind Mikey.
E nergetic Mikey.
Y ay! I love Mikey.

Chloe Kearsley (5)
The Gates Primary School, Westhoughton

Park

P lay with my friends at the park.
A dventures for all.
R unning on the track.
K icking about.

Junior James McWhinnie (6)
The Gates Primary School, Westhoughton

Wonderful World Of Belle

B eautiful girl.
E nergetic girl.
L ittle girl.
L ikes all of us.
E xciting girl.

George Shaw (5)
The Gates Primary School, Westhoughton

Bouncing Bunty

B ouncing Bunty.
U nusual hair.
N ice and smiley.
T iny guinea pig.
Y oung.

Emily Fletcher (5)
The Gates Primary School, Westhoughton

Wonderful World Of Bella

B eautiful hair.
E nergetic and fast.
L ies down.
L ikes
A wesome love.

Harry Mylrea (5)
The Gates Primary School, Westhoughton

Lexi

L exi is funny, she makes me laugh.
E xcellent Lexi.
e **X** citing Lexi.
I love Lexi.

Amelia Eaves (6)
The Gates Primary School, Westhoughton

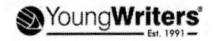

Jinxy The Cat

J inxy watches you play.
I tchy.
N ice.
e **X** cellent.
Y our cat sneezes.

Caitlin Emelia Holden-Green (5)
The Gates Primary School, Westhoughton

Max The Sausage Dog

M ax likes to roll down the stairs.
A sausage dog.
e **X** cellent brown dog.

Zakariya Jones (5)
The Gates Primary School, Westhoughton

Seaside, My Favourite Place

S easide is by the sea, and it's my favourite.
E xperience it and you will love it.
A lot of people visit every year.
S ometimes in the summer or early winter.
I t's really gorgeous.
D ay or night, it is amazing.
E veryone's favourite, but I love it the most!

Brianna Olaniyi-Edwards (6)
Woodlands School, Great Warley

Ice Cream

I ce is freezing cold.
C ream is smooth.
E arth is geographic.

C assie is in Year Two.
R unning is a sport.
E ggs can be boiled.
A baby hedgehog is a hoglet.
M y mummy is an adult.

Lucas Oluitan (6)
Woodlands School, Great Warley

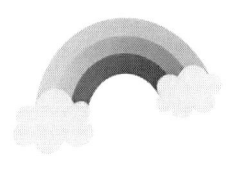

Aaron

A aron is my best brother.
A maya is my brother's sister.
R unning in the garden.
O MG! It's my brother.
N aughty, but nice.

Arya Patel (6)
Woodlands School, Great Warley

Nectarine

N ectarines grow on trees.
E veryone like nectarines, they are juicy.
C overed in lovely orange skin.
T astier than oranges.
A fter they are picked you can buy them in a shop.
R eally yummy for a snack.
I n your tummy, they are really good.
N ectarines are yummy to eat.
E ven in a fruit salad.

William Marx (5)
Woodlands School Hutton Manor, Hutton

My Amazing Style

S parkly shoes, I like to wear.
T wirly ballet, I dance in my pink tutu.
Y oga is when I wear comfy clothes.
L ove to braid my hair when I dress like a princess.
I n my hair, I wear rainbow bows.
S potty dresses, blue and white.
H ealthy food is what I like to eat, but ice cream is my favourite treat.

Mia Isabel Jordan (6)
Woodlands School Hutton Manor, Hutton

Broccoli

B umpy broccoli is healthy and tasty.
R aw broccoli is not very nice.
O n a plate looking bright and green.
C urly and green like little trees.
C ook them in a pan.
O n my roast it is yummy.
L unch or dinner, you can eat it any time.
I t's a very tasty treat.

Thomas Howells (5)
Woodlands School Hutton Manor, Hutton

Theatre

T he theatre is ready for action.
H ere in the audience, there are lots of people.
E at lots of ice cream in the interval.
A ctors are ready to sing and dance.
T ime to open the curtains.
R ehearsals are finished now.
E very show, everyone is excited.

Annie Barke (6)
Woodlands School Hutton Manor, Hutton

Holiday

H otel Serena Blue is massive.
O ur swimming pool was big.
L ove mum and dad lots.
I like going on the plane.
D rinking apple juice is wonderful.
A girl called Lola is my friend.
Y ellow sun was shining.

Heath Lenz (6)
Woodlands School Hutton Manor, Hutton

Hannah

H annah is my mummy
A nd my favourite in the family.
N ice and cuddleable.
N uts are her favourite food.
A crunchy apple she likes to munch.
H appy mummy.

Beth Currie (6)
Woodlands School Hutton Manor, Hutton

Nanny

N anny is lovely and kind.
A nother treat if I say please.
N ot another game show!
N early sixty-six years married but
Y oung at heart.

Penelope Kettle (6)
Woodlands School Hutton Manor, Hutton

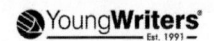

Apple

A pples grow in orchards.
P eople love to eat them in pies.
P lenty of red, green and pink.
L ovely and juicy.
E xtra crunch for you.

Zachary Hill (5)
Woodlands School Hutton Manor, Hutton

Jamie

J aguars are rough.
A pes eat bananas.
M onkeys are naughty.
I like my toys.
E very day I do science.

Jamie Murphy (6)
Woodlands School Hutton Manor, Hutton

Heart

H ugs and kisses.
E veryone loves them.
A sign of love.
R ound at the top.
T hey are red and pink.

Florence Bray (7)
Woodlands School Hutton Manor, Hutton

Bella

B ig bones.
E verything she eats.
L aying in the sun.
L oving all the fun.
A nd Bella is our baby.

Scarlett George (6)
Woodlands School Hutton Manor, Hutton

Dog

D ogs are big.
O r dogs can be small.
G oing on walks to exercise dogs.

Harry Carr (7)
Woodlands School Hutton Manor, Hutton

Young Writers Information

We hope you have enjoyed reading this book – and that you will continue to in the coming years.

If you're a young writer who enjoys reading and creative writing, or the parent of an enthusiastic poet or story writer, do visit our website **www.youngwriters.co.uk**. Here you will find free competitions, workshops and games, as well as recommended reads, a poetry glossary and our blog. There's lots to keep budding writers motivated to write!

If you would like to order further copies of this book, or any of our other titles, then please give us a call or order via your online account.

Young Writers
Remus House
Coltsfoot Drive
Peterborough
PE2 9BF
(01733) 890066
info@youngwriters.co.uk

Join in the conversation!
Tips, news, giveaways and much more!

YoungWritersUK   @YoungWritersCW